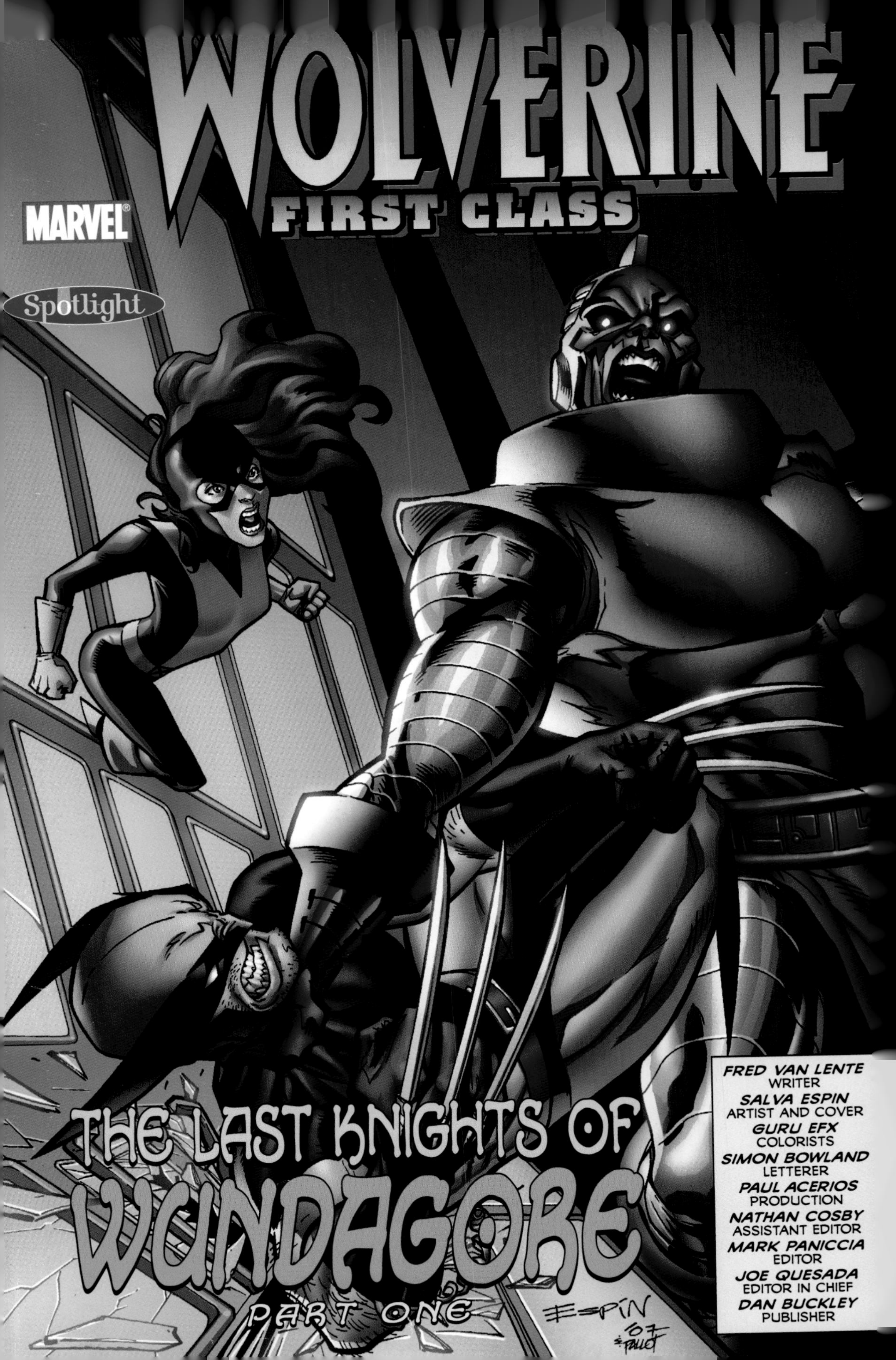
WOLVERINE
FIRST CLASS
MARVEL
Spotlight
THE LAST KNIGHTS OF
WUNDAGORE
PART ONE
FRED VAN LENTE
WRITER
SALVA ESPIN
ARTIST AND COVER
GURU EFX
COLORISTS
SIMON BOWLAND
LETTERER
PAUL ACERIOS
PRODUCTION
NATHAN COSBY
ASSISTANT EDITOR
MARK PANICCIA
EDITOR
JOE QUESADA
EDITOR IN CHIEF
DAN BUCKLEY
PUBLISHER

VISIT US AT
www.abdopublishing.com

Reinforced library bound edition published in 2010 by Spotlight, a division of the ABDO Group, 8000 West 78th Street, Edina, Minnesota 55439. Spotlight produces high-quality reinforced library bound editions for schools and libraries. Published by agreement with Marvel Characters, Inc.

Library of Congress Cataloging-in-Publication Data

Van Lente, Fred.
  The last knights of Wundagore. Part 1 / Fred Van Lente, writer ; Salva Espin, artist & cover ; Guru eFX, colorists ; Simon Bowland, letterer. -- Reinforced library bound ed.
     p. cm. -- (Wolverine, first class)
  "Marvel."
  ISBN 978-1-59961-671-1
  1. Graphic novels. 2. Graphic novels. [1. Graphic novels. 2. Superheroes--Fiction.] I. Espin, Salva, ill. II. Bowland, Simon. III. Guru eFX (Firm) IV. Title.
  PZ7.7.V26Las 2009
  741.5'973--dc22

                              2009010136

All Spotlight books have reinforced library bindings and are manufactured in the United States of America.

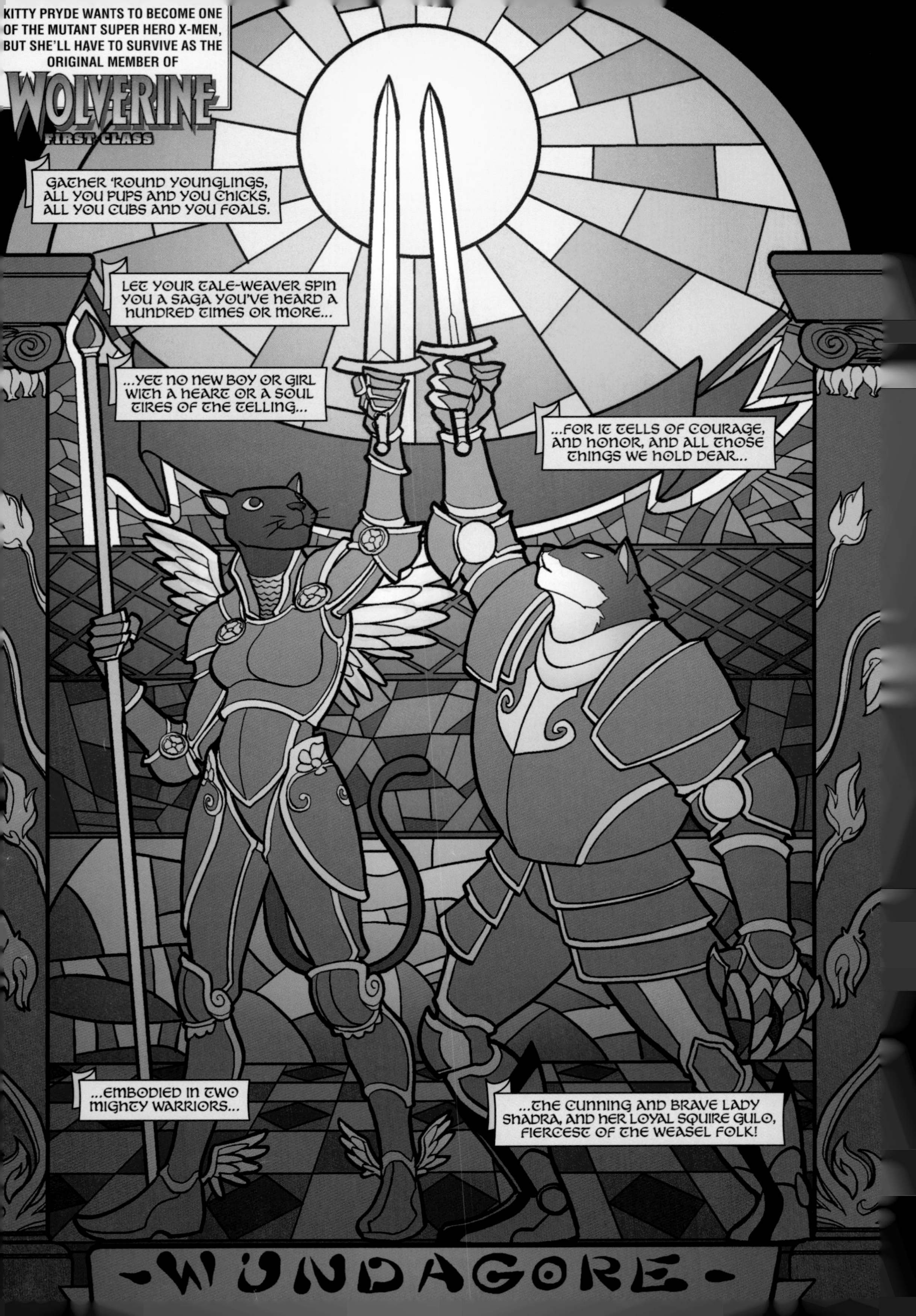
KITTY PRYDE WANTS TO BECOME ONE OF THE MUTANT SUPER HERO X-MEN, BUT SHE'LL HAVE TO SURVIVE AS THE ORIGINAL MEMBER OF
WOLVERINE
FIRST CLASS
GATHER 'ROUND YOUNGLINGS, ALL YOU PUPS AND YOU CHICKS, ALL YOU CUBS AND YOU FOALS.
LET YOUR TALE-WEAVER SPIN YOU A SAGA YOU'VE HEARD A HUNDRED TIMES OR MORE...
...YET NO NEW BOY OR GIRL WITH A HEART OR A SOUL TIRES OF THE TELLING...
...FOR IT TELLS OF COURAGE, AND HONOR, AND ALL THOSE THINGS WE HOLD DEAR...
...EMBODIED IN TWO MIGHTY WARRIORS...
...THE CUNNING AND BRAVE LADY SHADRA, AND HER LOYAL SQUIRE GULO, FIERCEST OF THE WEASEL FOLK!
-WUNDAGORE-

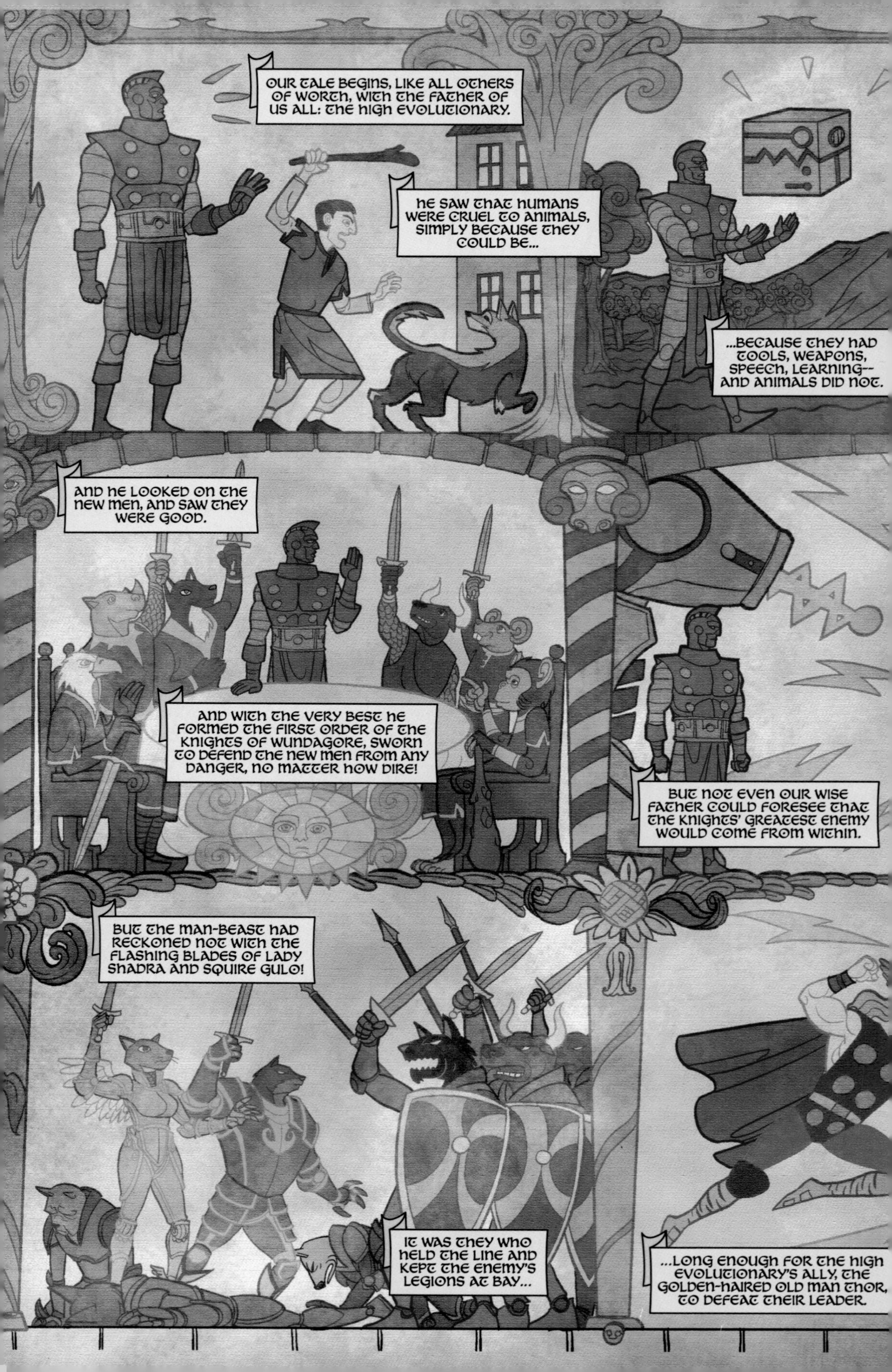
OUR TALE BEGINS, LIKE ALL OTHERS OF WORTH, WITH THE FATHER OF US ALL: THE HIGH EVOLUTIONARY.
HE SAW THAT HUMANS WERE CRUEL TO ANIMALS, SIMPLY BECAUSE THEY COULD BE...
...BECAUSE THEY HAD TOOLS, WEAPONS, SPEECH, LEARNING--AND ANIMALS DID NOT.
AND HE LOOKED ON THE NEW MEN, AND SAW THEY WERE GOOD.
AND WITH THE VERY BEST HE FORMED THE FIRST ORDER OF THE KNIGHTS OF WUNDAGORE, SWORN TO DEFEND THE NEW MEN FROM ANY DANGER, NO MATTER HOW DIRE!
BUT NOT EVEN OUR WISE FATHER COULD FORESEE THAT THE KNIGHTS' GREATEST ENEMY WOULD COME FROM WITHIN.
BUT THE MAN-BEAST HAD RECKONED NOT WITH THE FLASHING BLADES OF LADY SHADRA AND SQUIRE GULO!
IT WAS THEY WHO HELD THE LINE AND KEPT THE ENEMY'S LEGIONS AT BAY...
...LONG ENOUGH FOR THE HIGH EVOLUTIONARY'S ALLY, THE GOLDEN-HAIRED OLD MAN THOR, TO DEFEAT THEIR LEADER.

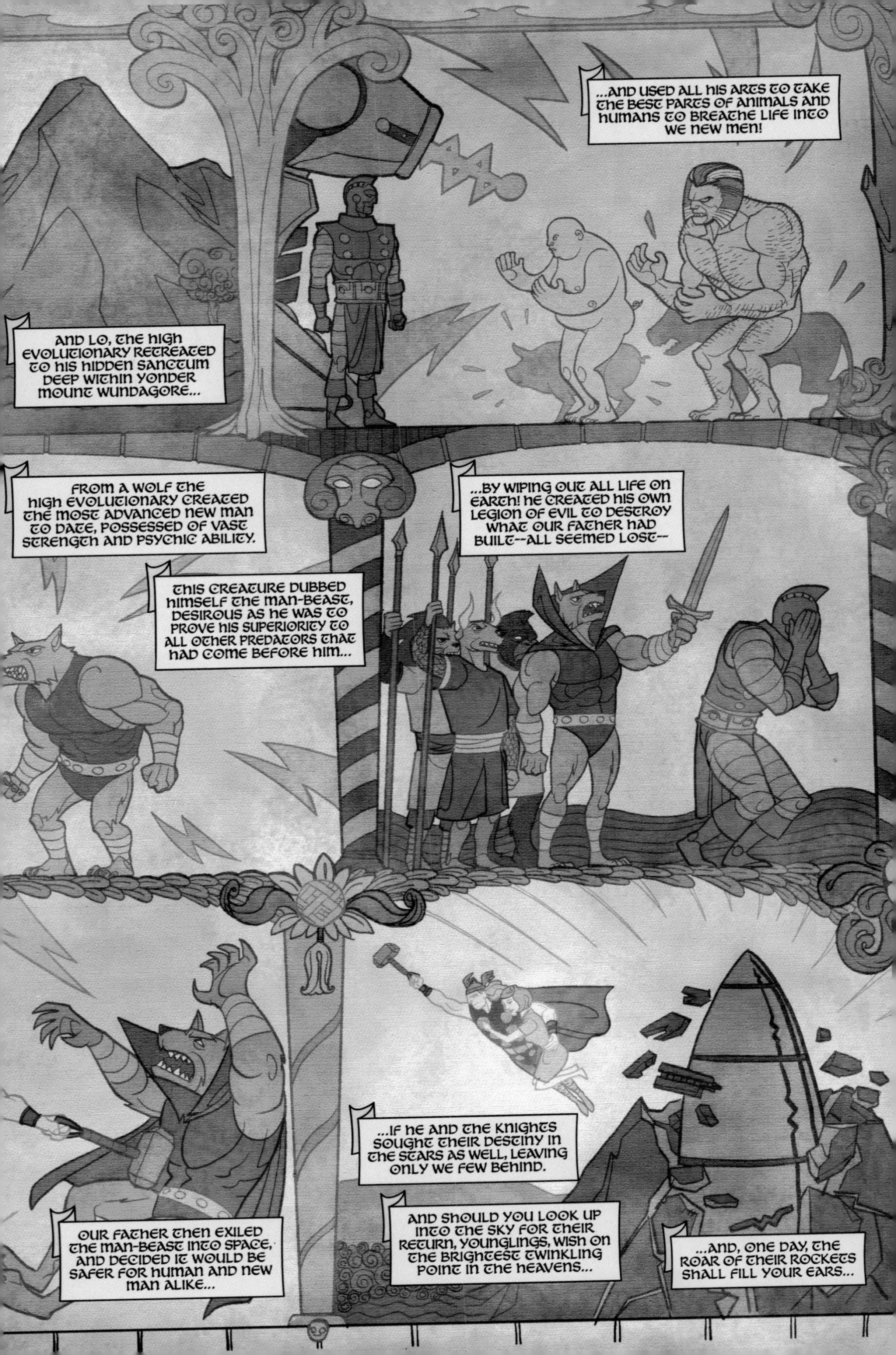
...AND USED ALL HIS ARTS TO TAKE THE BEST PARTS OF ANIMALS AND HUMANS TO BREATHE LIFE INTO WE NEW MEN!
AND LO, THE HIGH EVOLUTIONARY RETREATED TO HIS HIDDEN SANCTUM DEEP WITHIN YONDER MOUNT WUNDAGORE...
FROM A WOLF THE HIGH EVOLUTIONARY CREATED THE MOST ADVANCED NEW MAN TO DATE, POSSESSED OF VAST STRENGTH AND PSYCHIC ABILITY.
THIS CREATURE DUBBED HIMSELF THE MAN-BEAST, DESIROUS AS HE WAS TO PROVE HIS SUPERIORITY TO ALL OTHER PREDATORS THAT HAD COME BEFORE HIM...
...BY WIPING OUT ALL LIFE ON EARTH! HE CREATED HIS OWN LEGION OF EVIL TO DESTROY WHAT OUR FATHER HAD BUILT--ALL SEEMED LOST--
OUR FATHER THEN EXILED THE MAN-BEAST INTO SPACE, AND DECIDED IT WOULD BE SAFER FOR HUMAN AND NEW MAN ALIKE...
...IF HE AND THE KNIGHTS SOUGHT THEIR DESTINY IN THE STARS AS WELL, LEAVING ONLY WE FEW BEHIND.
AND SHOULD YOU LOOK UP INTO THE SKY FOR THEIR RETURN, YOUNGLINGS, WISH ON THE BRIGHTEST TWINKLING POINT IN THE HEAVENS...
...AND, ONE DAY, THE ROAR OF THEIR ROCKETS SHALL FILL YOUR EARS...

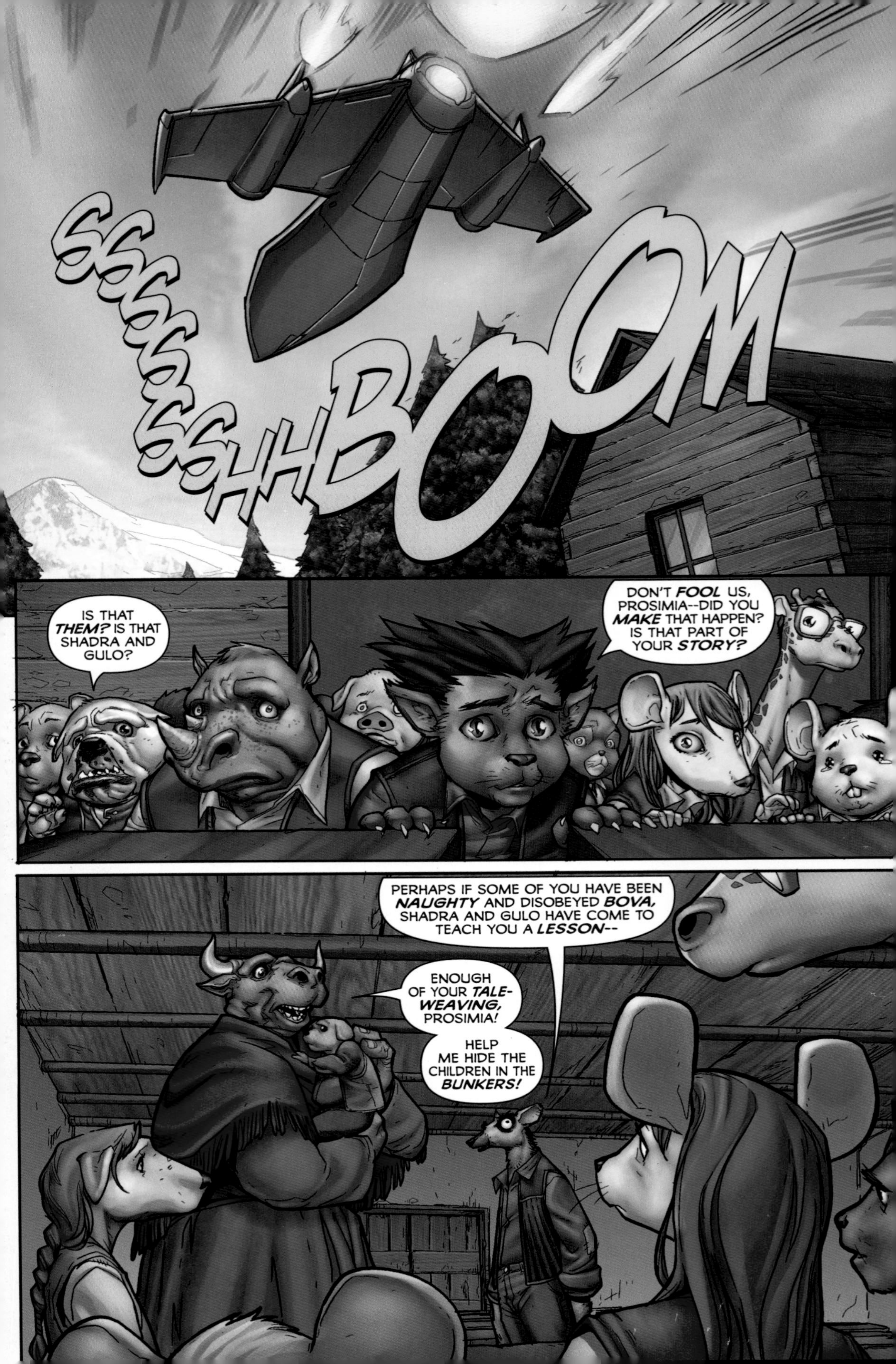
SSSSSSSHBOOM
IS THAT THEM? IS THAT SHADRA AND GULO?
DON'T FOOL US, PROSIMIA--DID YOU MAKE THAT HAPPEN? IS THAT PART OF YOUR STORY?
PERHAPS IF SOME OF YOU HAVE BEEN NAUGHTY AND DISOBEYED BOVA, SHADRA AND GULO HAVE COME TO TEACH YOU A LESSON--
ENOUGH OF YOUR TALE-WEAVING, PROSIMIA!
HELP ME HIDE THE CHILDREN IN THE BUNKERS!

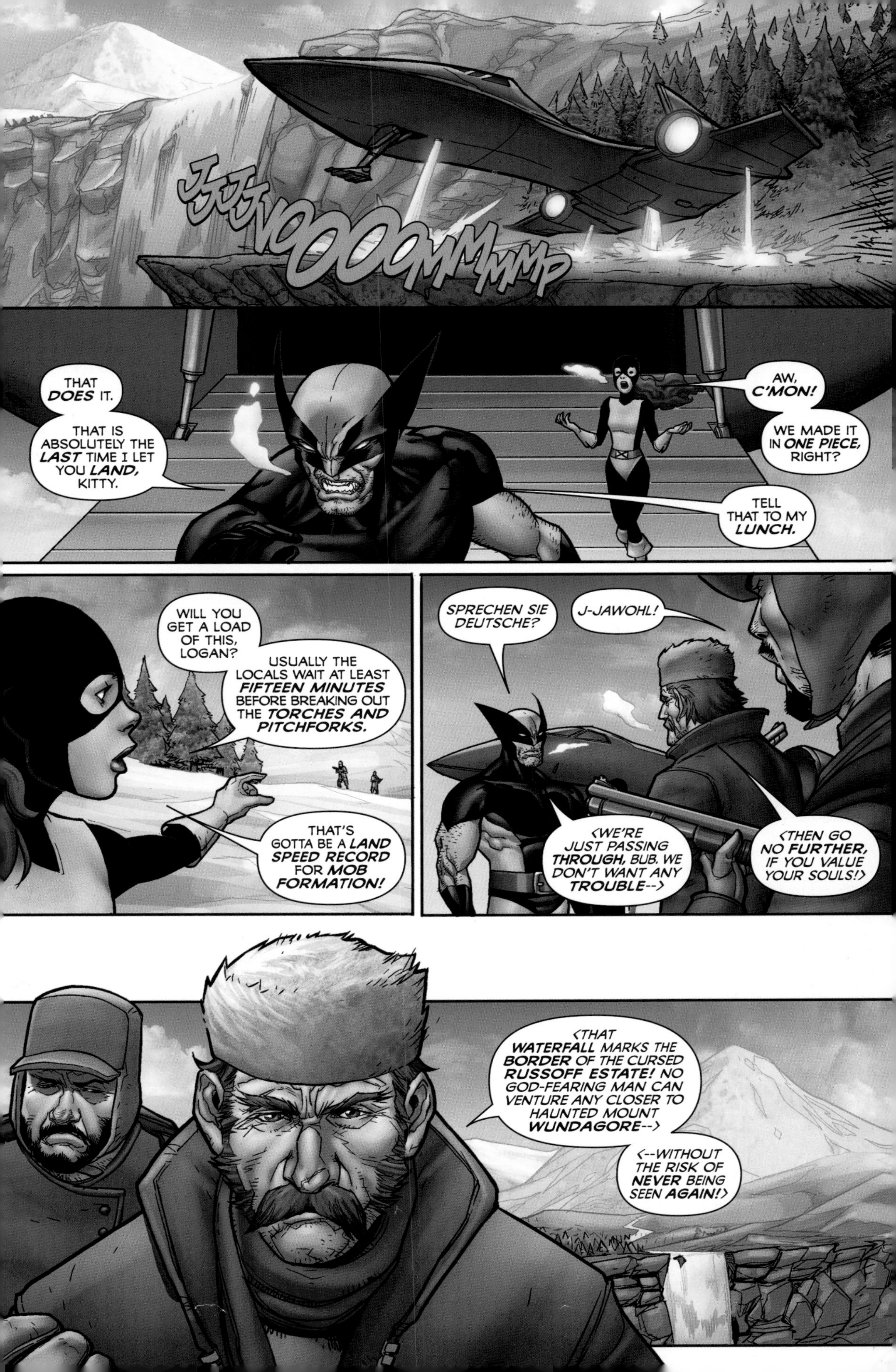
JJJJVOOOOMMMMP
THAT DOES IT.
THAT IS ABSOLUTELY THE LAST TIME I LET YOU LAND, KITTY.
AW, C'MON!
WE MADE IT IN ONE PIECE, RIGHT?
TELL THAT TO MY LUNCH.
WILL YOU GET A LOAD OF THIS, LOGAN?
USUALLY THE LOCALS WAIT AT LEAST FIFTEEN MINUTES BEFORE BREAKING OUT THE TORCHES AND PITCHFORKS.
THAT'S GOTTA BE A LAND SPEED RECORD FOR MOB FORMATION!
SPRECHEN SIE DEUTSCHE?
J-JAWOHL!
<WE'RE JUST PASSING THROUGH, BUB. WE DON'T WANT ANY TROUBLE-->
<THEN GO NO FURTHER, IF YOU VALUE YOUR SOULS!>
<THAT WATERFALL MARKS THE BORDER OF THE CURSED RUSSOFF ESTATE! NO GOD-FEARING MAN CAN VENTURE ANY CLOSER TO HAUNTED MOUNT WUNDAGORE-->
<--WITHOUT THE RISK OF NEVER BEING SEEN AGAIN!>

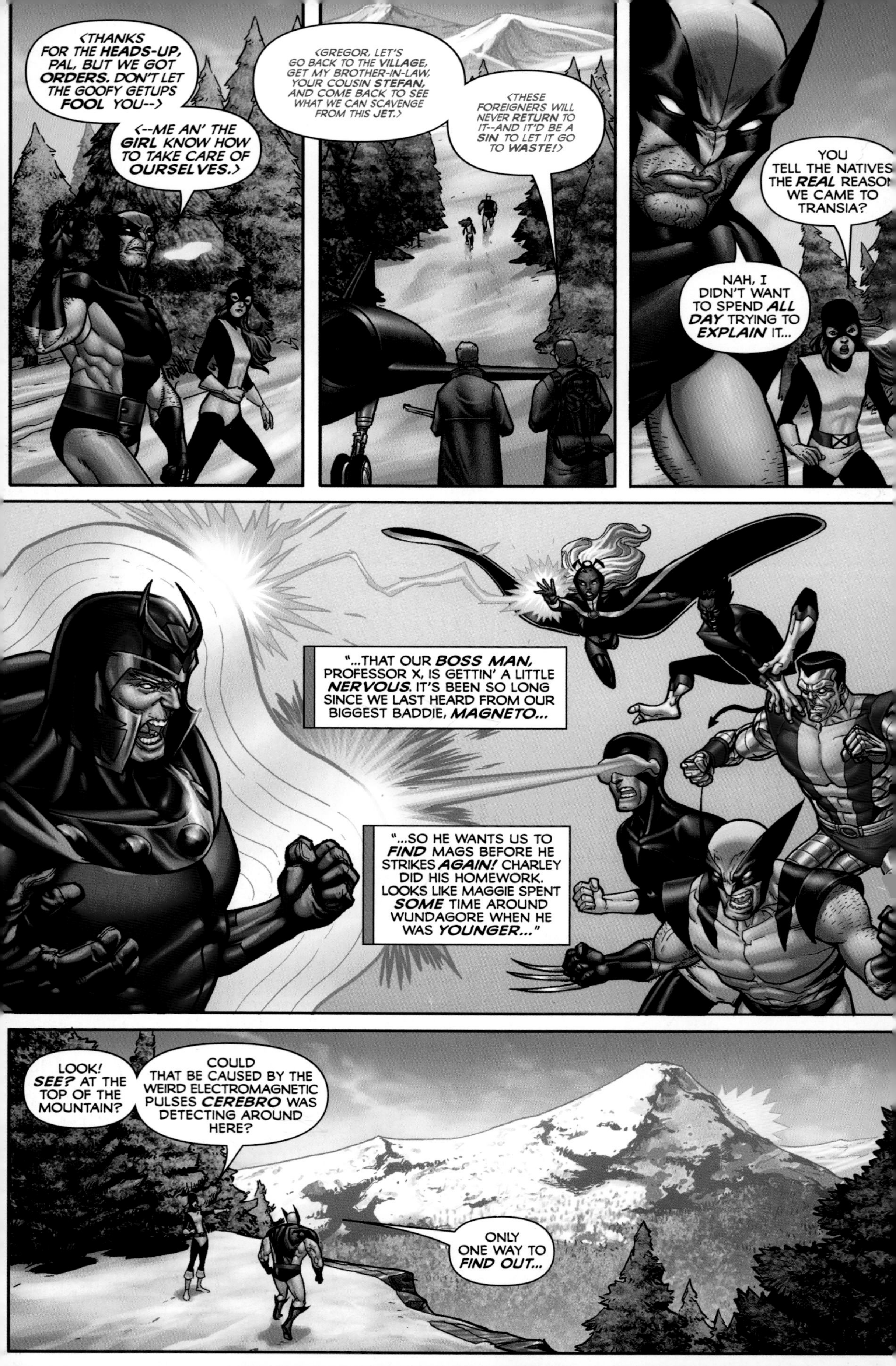

<THANKS FOR THE HEADS-UP, PAL, BUT WE GOT ORDERS. DON'T LET THE GOOFY GETUPS FOOL YOU-->
<--ME AN' THE GIRL KNOW HOW TO TAKE CARE OF OURSELVES.>
<GREGOR, LET'S GO BACK TO THE VILLAGE, GET MY BROTHER-IN-LAW, YOUR COUSIN STEFAN, AND COME BACK TO SEE WHAT WE CAN SCAVENGE FROM THIS JET.>
<THESE FOREIGNERS WILL NEVER RETURN TO IT--AND IT'D BE A SIN TO LET IT GO TO WASTE!>
YOU TELL THE NATIVES THE REAL REASON WE CAME TO TRANSIA?
NAH, I DIDN'T WANT TO SPEND ALL DAY TRYING TO EXPLAIN IT...
"...THAT OUR BOSS MAN, PROFESSOR X, IS GETTIN' A LITTLE NERVOUS. IT'S BEEN SO LONG SINCE WE LAST HEARD FROM OUR BIGGEST BADDIE, MAGNETO...
"...SO HE WANTS US TO FIND MAGS BEFORE HE STRIKES AGAIN! CHARLEY DID HIS HOMEWORK. LOOKS LIKE MAGGIE SPENT SOME TIME AROUND WUNDAGORE WHEN HE WAS YOUNGER..."
LOOK! SEE? AT THE TOP OF THE MOUNTAIN?
COULD THAT BE CAUSED BY THE WEIRD ELECTROMAGNETIC PULSES CEREBRO WAS DETECTING AROUND HERE?
ONLY ONE WAY TO FIND OUT...

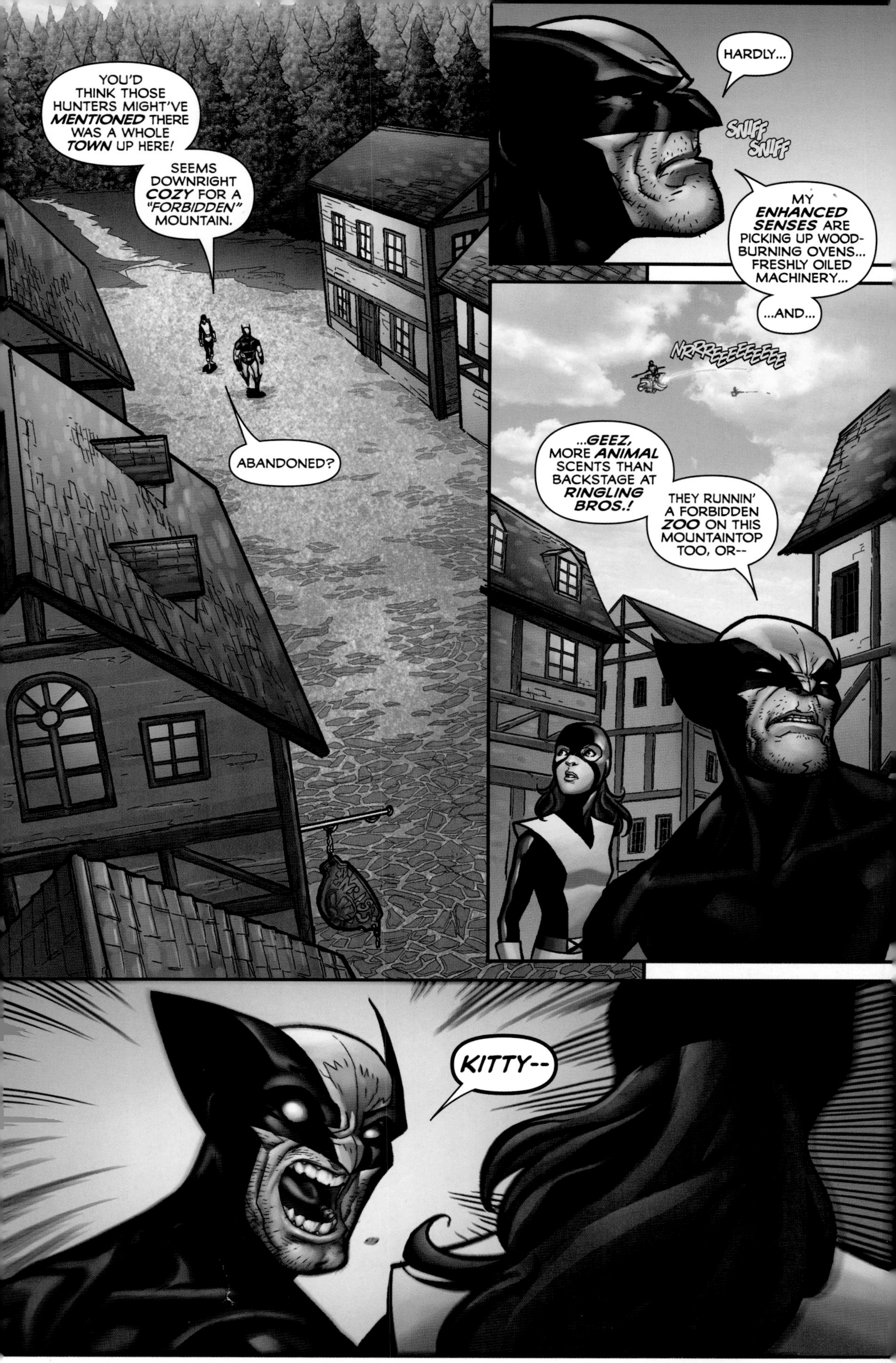
YOU'D THINK THOSE HUNTERS MIGHT'VE MENTIONED THERE WAS A WHOLE TOWN UP HERE!
SEEMS DOWNRIGHT COZY FOR A "FORBIDDEN" MOUNTAIN.
ABANDONED?
HARDLY...
SNIFF SNIFF
MY ENHANCED SENSES ARE PICKING UP WOOD-BURNING OVENS... FRESHLY OILED MACHINERY...
...AND...
NRRREEEEEEEEE
...GEEZ, MORE ANIMAL SCENTS THAN BACKSTAGE AT RINGLING BROS.!
THEY RUNNIN' A FORBIDDEN ZOO ON THIS MOUNTAINTOP TOO, OR--
KITTY--

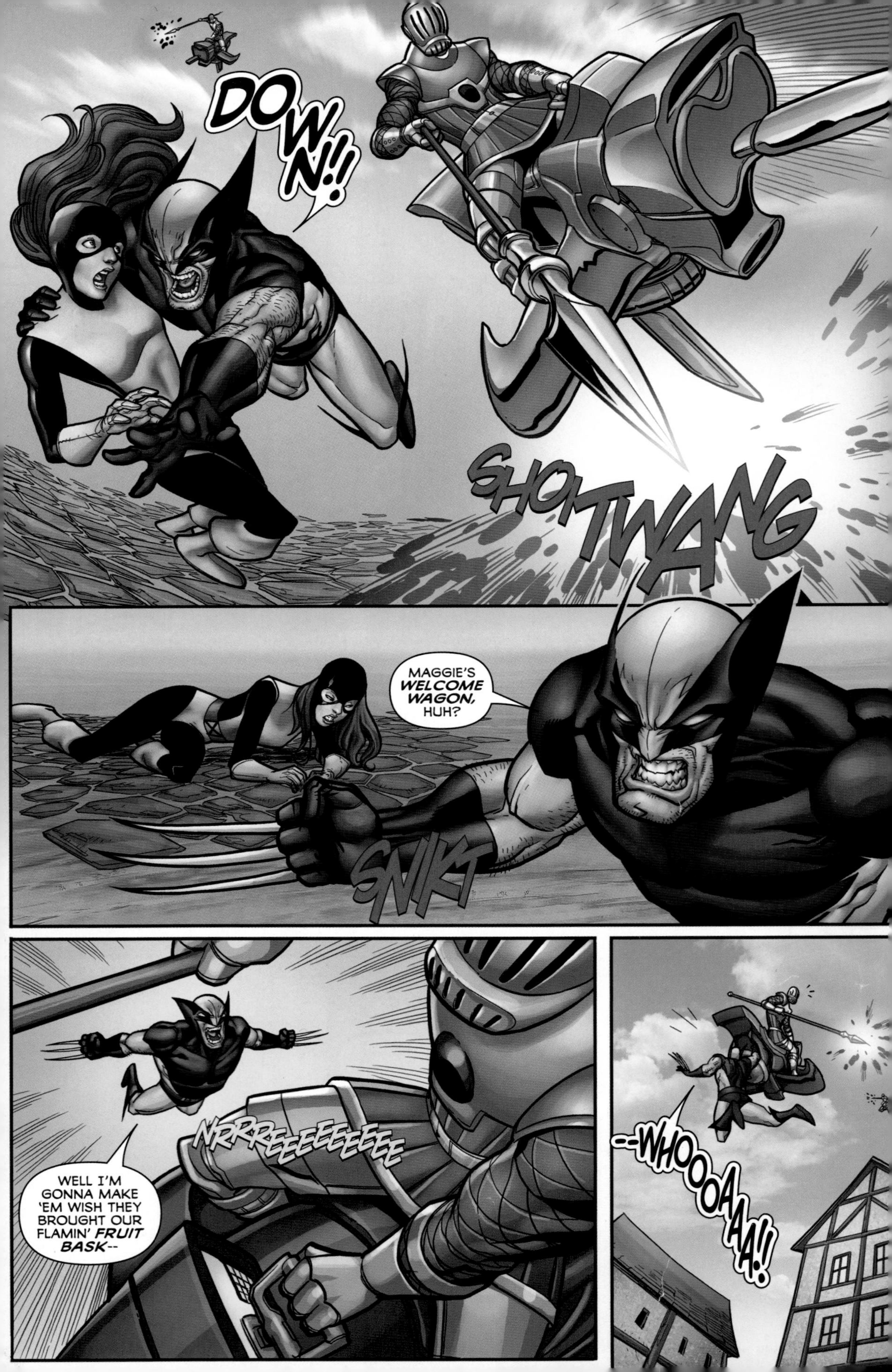
DOWN!!
SHOOM
TWANG
MAGGIE'S *WELCOME WAGON,* HUH?
SNIKT
NRRREEEEEEEEEE
WELL I'M GONNA MAKE 'EM WISH THEY BROUGHT OUR FLAMIN' *FRUIT BASK*--
--WHOOOAAA!!

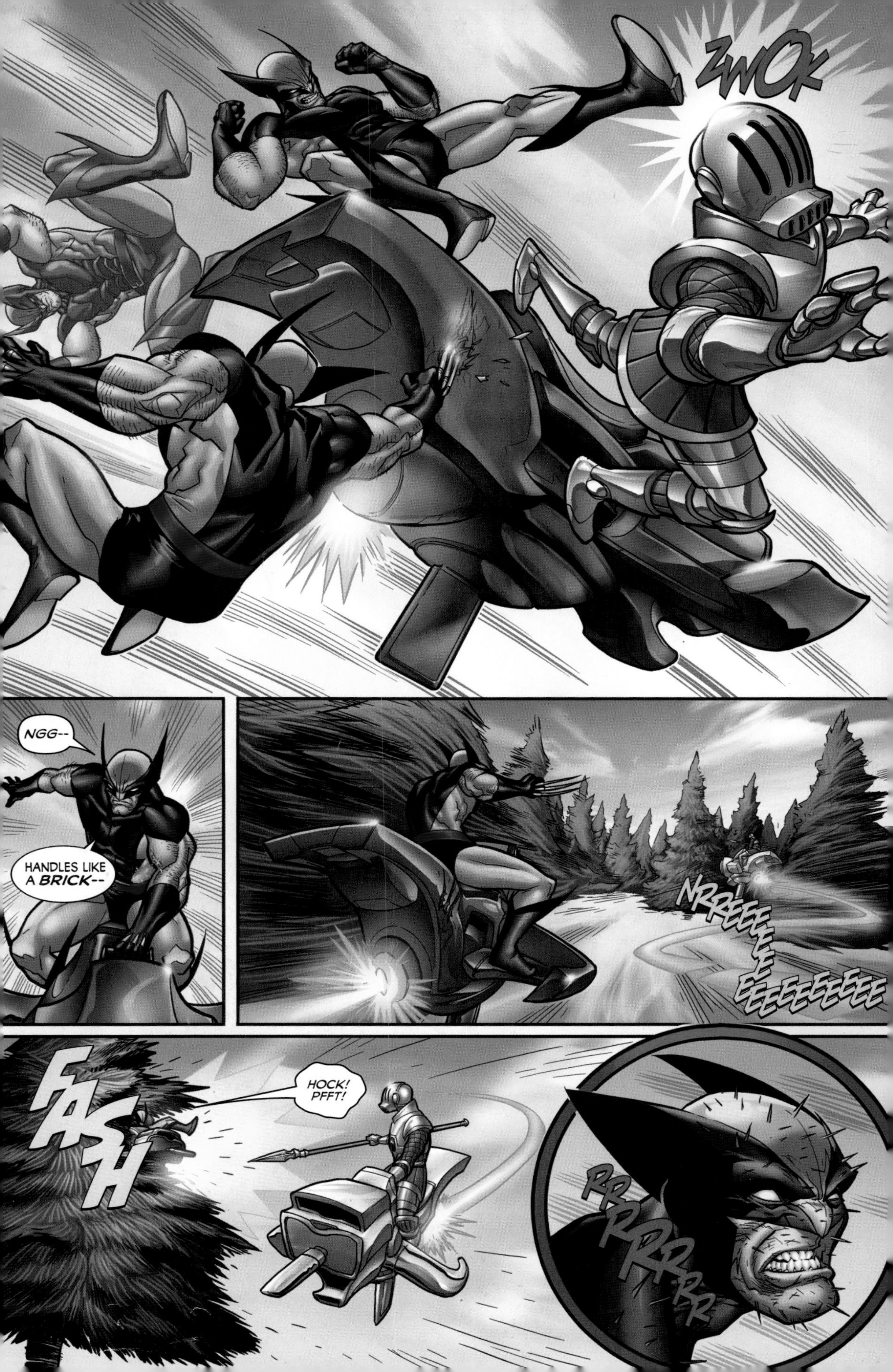
ZWOK
NGG--
HANDLES LIKE A BRICK--
NRREEEEEEEEEEEEEEEE
FASH
HOCK! PFFT!
RRRRRRRR

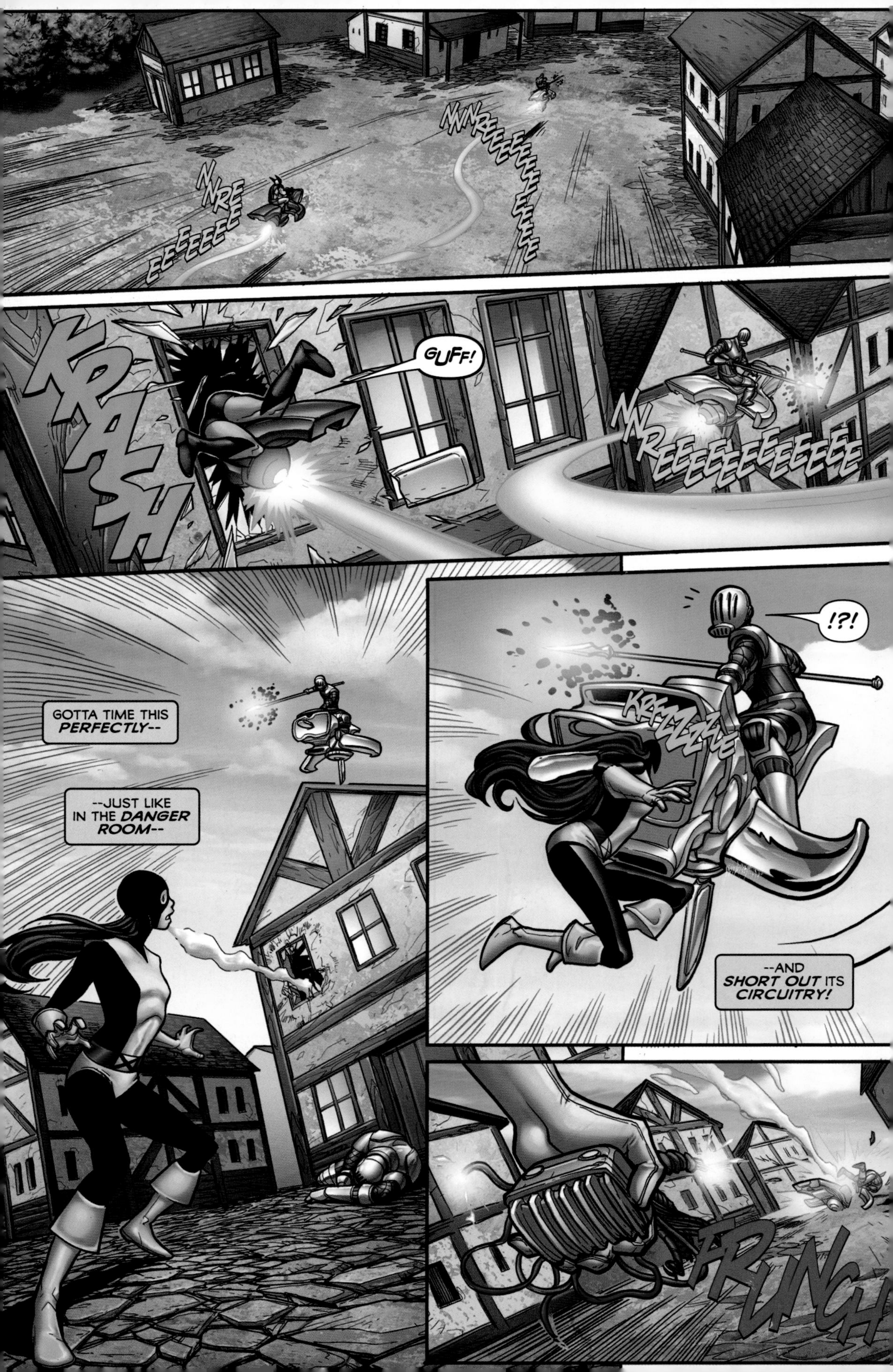

NNRE EEEEEEE
NNNREEEEEEEEEEEEEE
KRASH
GUFF!
NNREEEEEEEEEEEEEEE
GOTTA TIME THIS PERFECTLY--
--JUST LIKE IN THE DANGER ROOM--
!?!
KRZZZZZE
--AND SHORT OUT ITS CIRCUITRY!
FRUNCH

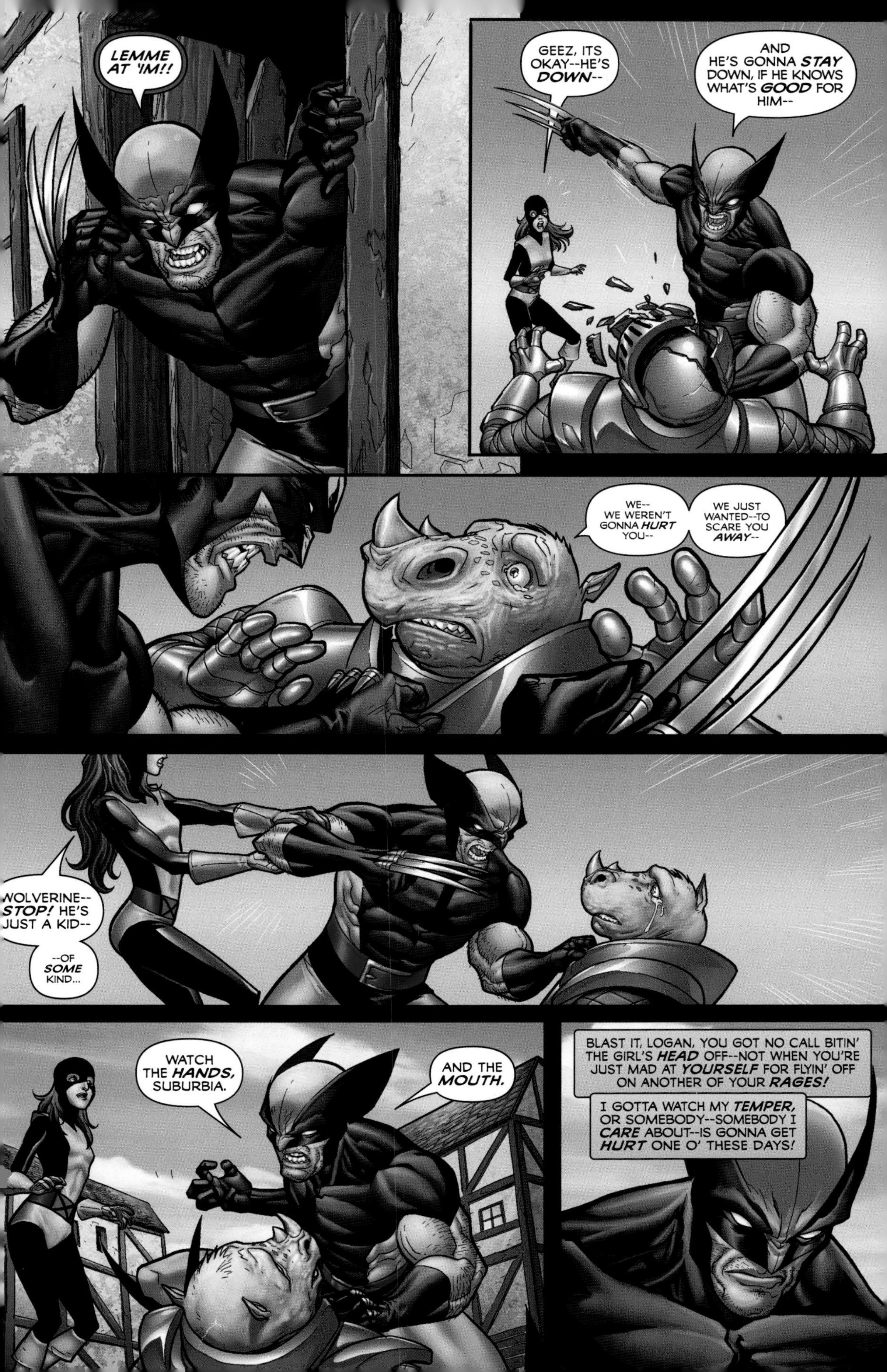
LEMME AT 'IM!!
GEEZ, ITS OKAY--HE'S *DOWN*--
AND HE'S GONNA *STAY* DOWN, IF HE KNOWS WHAT'S *GOOD* FOR HIM--
WE-- WE WEREN'T GONNA *HURT* YOU--
WE JUST WANTED--TO SCARE YOU *AWAY*--
WOLVERINE-- *STOP!* HE'S JUST A KID--
--OF *SOME* KIND...
WATCH THE *HANDS,* SUBURBIA.
AND THE *MOUTH.*
BLAST IT, LOGAN, YOU GOT NO CALL BITIN' THE GIRL'S *HEAD* OFF--NOT WHEN YOU'RE JUST MAD AT *YOURSELF* FOR FLYIN' OFF ON ANOTHER OF YOUR *RAGES!*
I GOTTA WATCH MY *TEMPER,* OR SOMEBODY--SOMEBODY I *CARE* ABOUT--IS GONNA GET *HURT* ONE O' THESE DAYS!

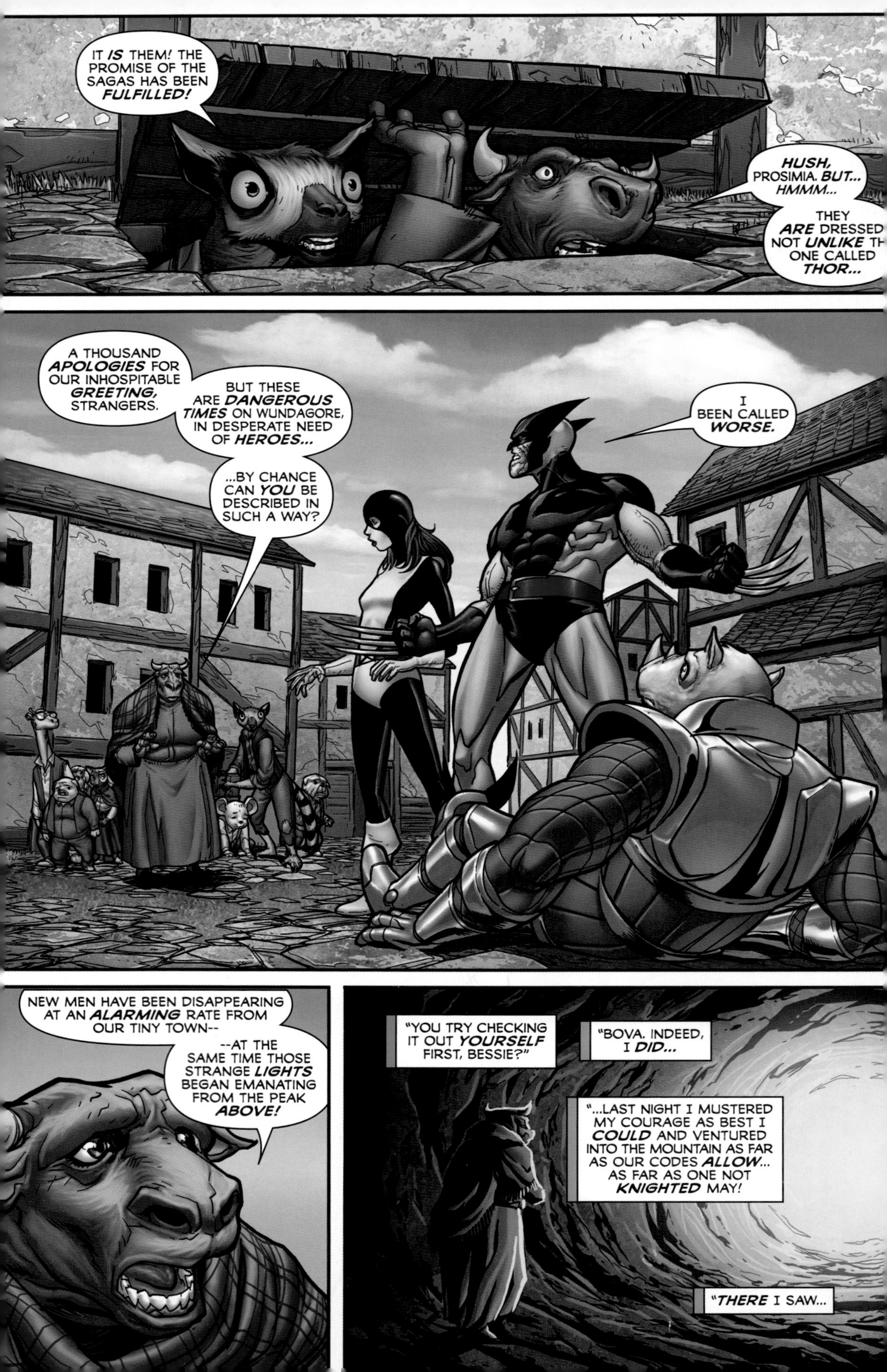
IT IS THEM! THE PROMISE OF THE SAGAS HAS BEEN FULFILLED!
HUSH, PROSIMIA. BUT... HMMM...
THEY ARE DRESSED NOT UNLIKE TH ONE CALLED THOR...
A THOUSAND APOLOGIES FOR OUR INHOSPITABLE GREETING, STRANGERS.
BUT THESE ARE DANGEROUS TIMES ON WUNDAGORE, IN DESPERATE NEED OF HEROES...
...BY CHANCE CAN YOU BE DESCRIBED IN SUCH A WAY?
I BEEN CALLED WORSE.
NEW MEN HAVE BEEN DISAPPEARING AT AN ALARMING RATE FROM OUR TINY TOWN--
--AT THE SAME TIME THOSE STRANGE LIGHTS BEGAN EMANATING FROM THE PEAK ABOVE!
"YOU TRY CHECKING IT OUT YOURSELF FIRST, BESSIE?"
"BOVA. INDEED, I DID...
"...LAST NIGHT I MUSTERED MY COURAGE AS BEST I COULD AND VENTURED INTO THE MOUNTAIN AS FAR AS OUR CODES ALLOW... AS FAR AS ONE NOT KNIGHTED MAY!
"THERE I SAW...

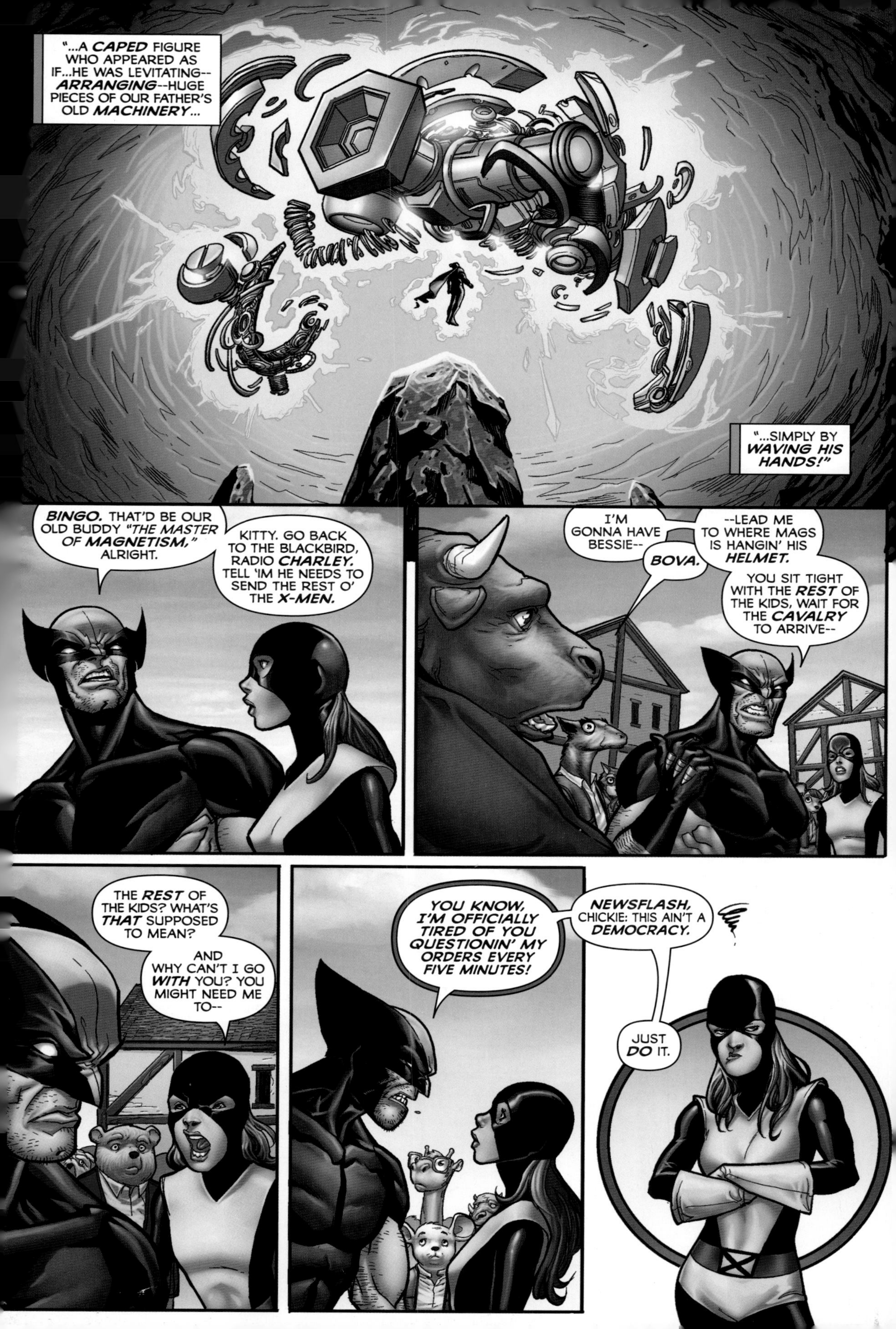
"...A CAPED FIGURE WHO APPEARED AS IF...HE WAS LEVITATING--ARRANGING--HUGE PIECES OF OUR FATHER'S OLD MACHINERY...
"...SIMPLY BY WAVING HIS HANDS!"
BINGO. THAT'D BE OUR OLD BUDDY "THE MASTER OF MAGNETISM," ALRIGHT.
KITTY. GO BACK TO THE BLACKBIRD, RADIO CHARLEY. TELL 'IM HE NEEDS TO SEND THE REST O' THE X-MEN.
I'M GONNA HAVE BESSIE--
BOVA.
--LEAD ME TO WHERE MAGS IS HANGIN' HIS HELMET.
YOU SIT TIGHT WITH THE REST OF THE KIDS, WAIT FOR THE CAVALRY TO ARRIVE--
THE REST OF THE KIDS? WHAT'S THAT SUPPOSED TO MEAN?
AND WHY CAN'T I GO WITH YOU? YOU MIGHT NEED ME TO--
YOU KNOW, I'M OFFICIALLY TIRED OF YOU QUESTIONIN' MY ORDERS EVERY FIVE MINUTES!
NEWSFLASH, CHICKIE: THIS AIN'T A DEMOCRACY.
JUST DO IT.

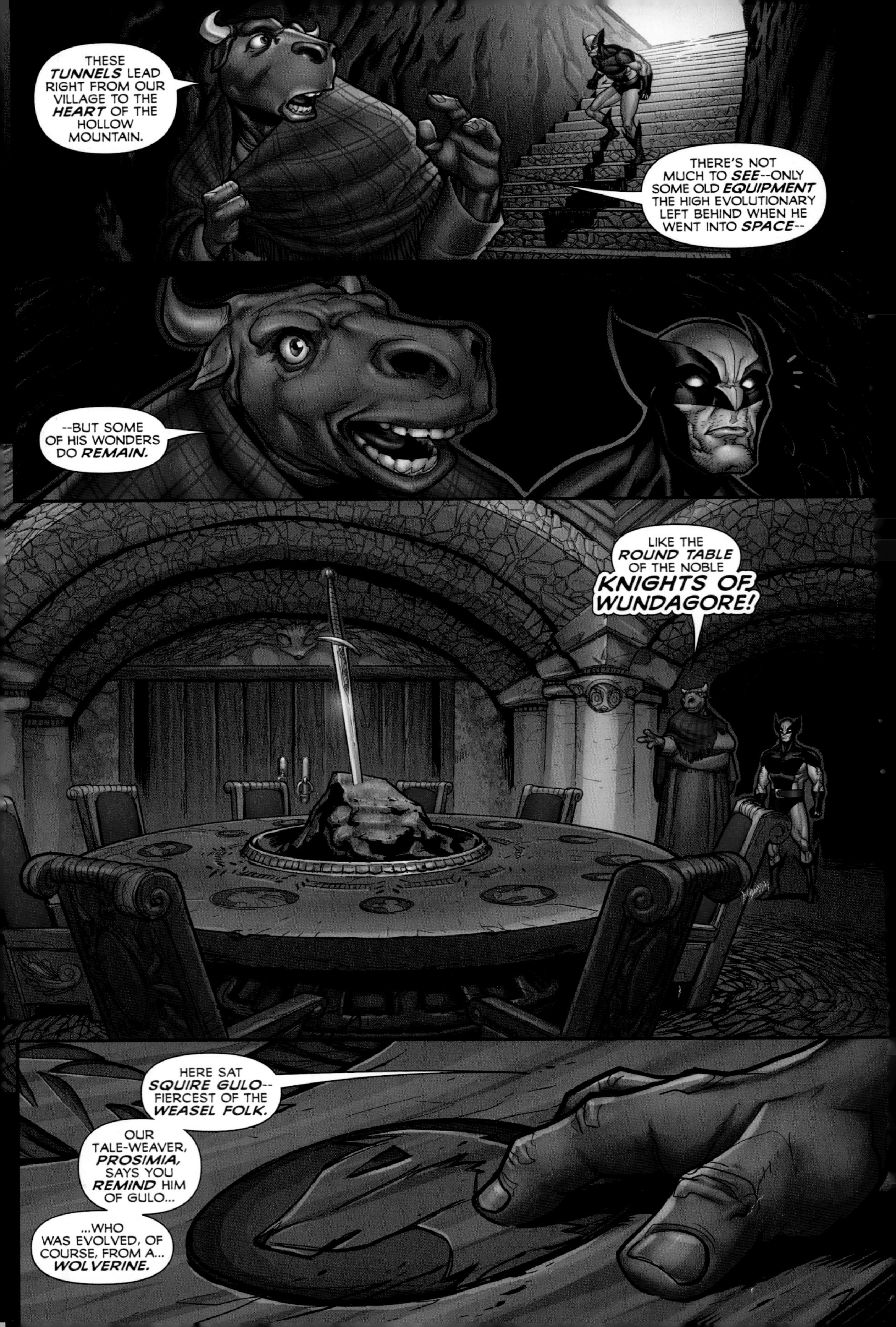

THESE TUNNELS LEAD RIGHT FROM OUR VILLAGE TO THE HEART OF THE HOLLOW MOUNTAIN.
THERE'S NOT MUCH TO SEE--ONLY SOME OLD EQUIPMENT THE HIGH EVOLUTIONARY LEFT BEHIND WHEN HE WENT INTO SPACE--
--BUT SOME OF HIS WONDERS DO REMAIN.
LIKE THE ROUND TABLE OF THE NOBLE KNIGHTS OF WUNDAGORE!
HERE SAT SQUIRE GULO--FIERCEST OF THE WEASEL FOLK.
OUR TALE-WEAVER, PROSIMIA, SAYS YOU REMIND HIM OF GULO...
...WHO WAS EVOLVED, OF COURSE, FROM A... WOLVERINE.

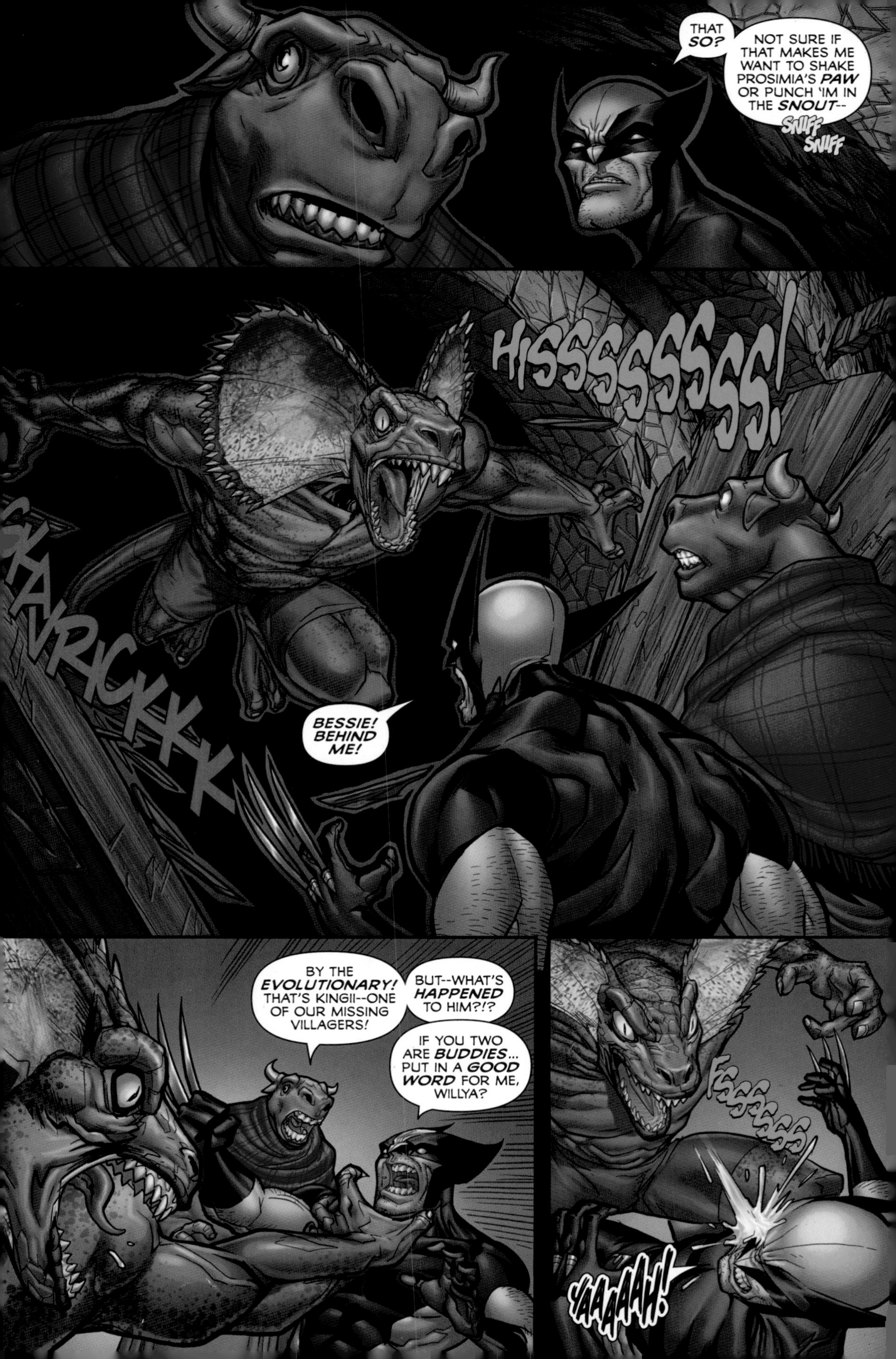

THAT SO?
NOT SURE IF THAT MAKES ME WANT TO SHAKE PROSIMIA'S PAW OR PUNCH 'IM IN THE SNOUT--
SNIFF SNIFF
HISSSSSSSSS!
SKRRICKKKK
BESSIE! BEHIND ME!
BY THE EVOLUTIONARY! THAT'S KINGII--ONE OF OUR MISSING VILLAGERS!
BUT--WHAT'S HAPPENED TO HIM?!?
IF YOU TWO ARE BUDDIES... PUT IN A GOOD WORD FOR ME, WILLYA?
FSSSSSSS
YAAAAAH!

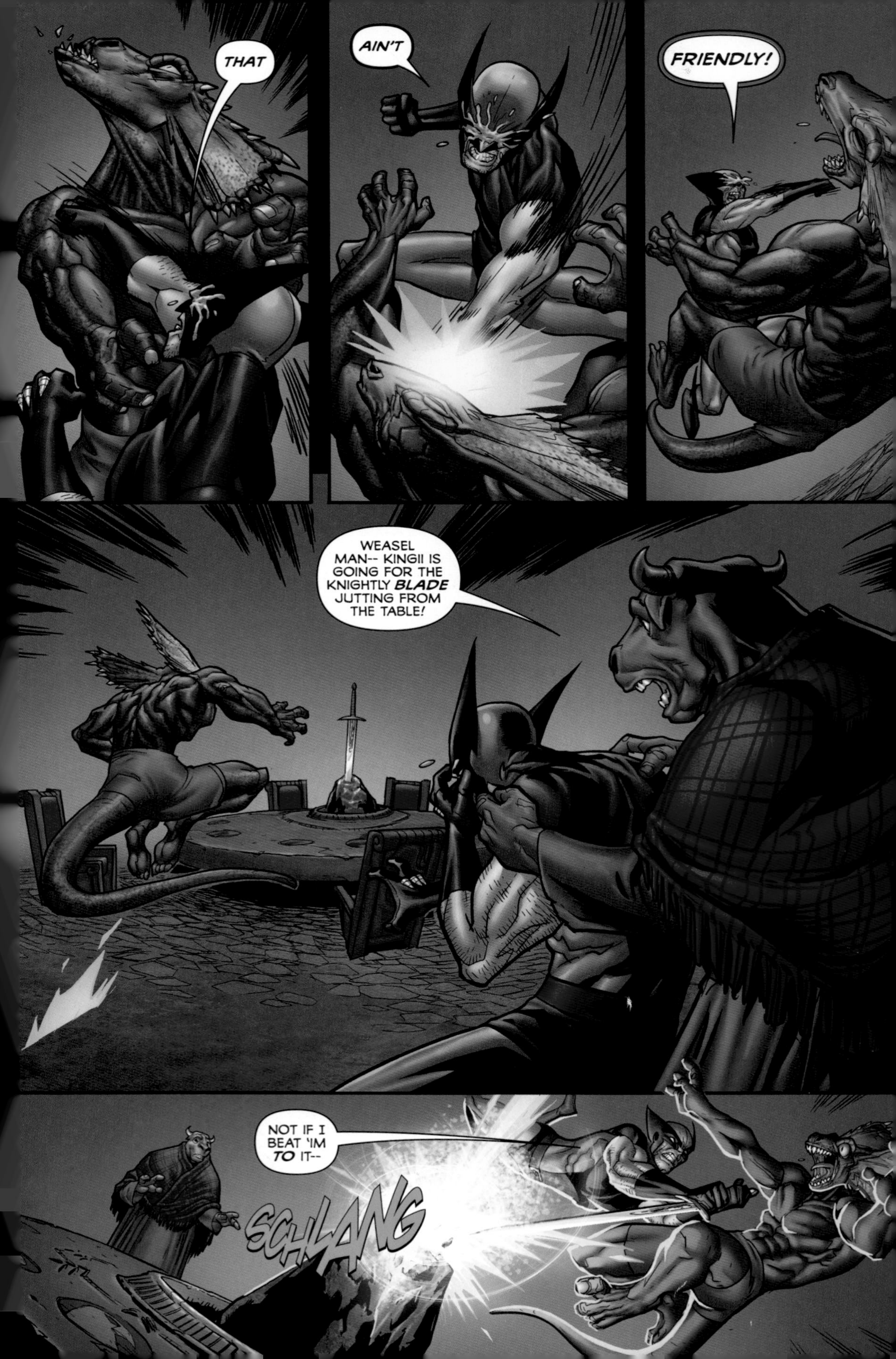
THAT
AIN'T
FRIENDLY!
WEASEL MAN-- KINGII IS GOING FOR THE KNIGHTLY *BLADE* JUTTING FROM THE TABLE!
NOT IF I BEAT 'IM *TO* IT--
SCHLANG

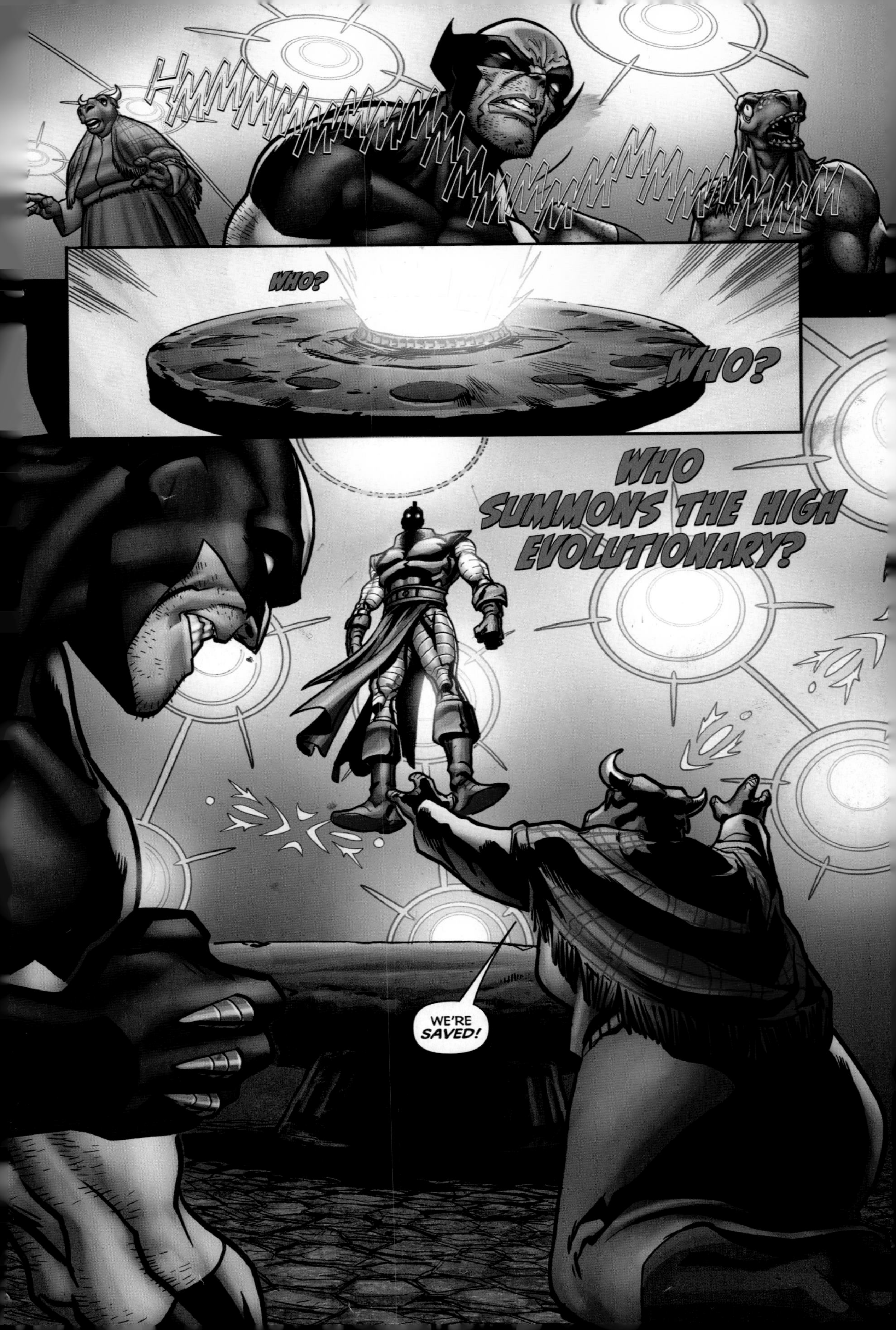
HMMMMMMMMMMMMMMMMMMMMMMMMMMMMMMMMM
WHO?
WHO?
WHO SUMMONS THE HIGH EVOLUTIONARY?
WE'RE SAVED!

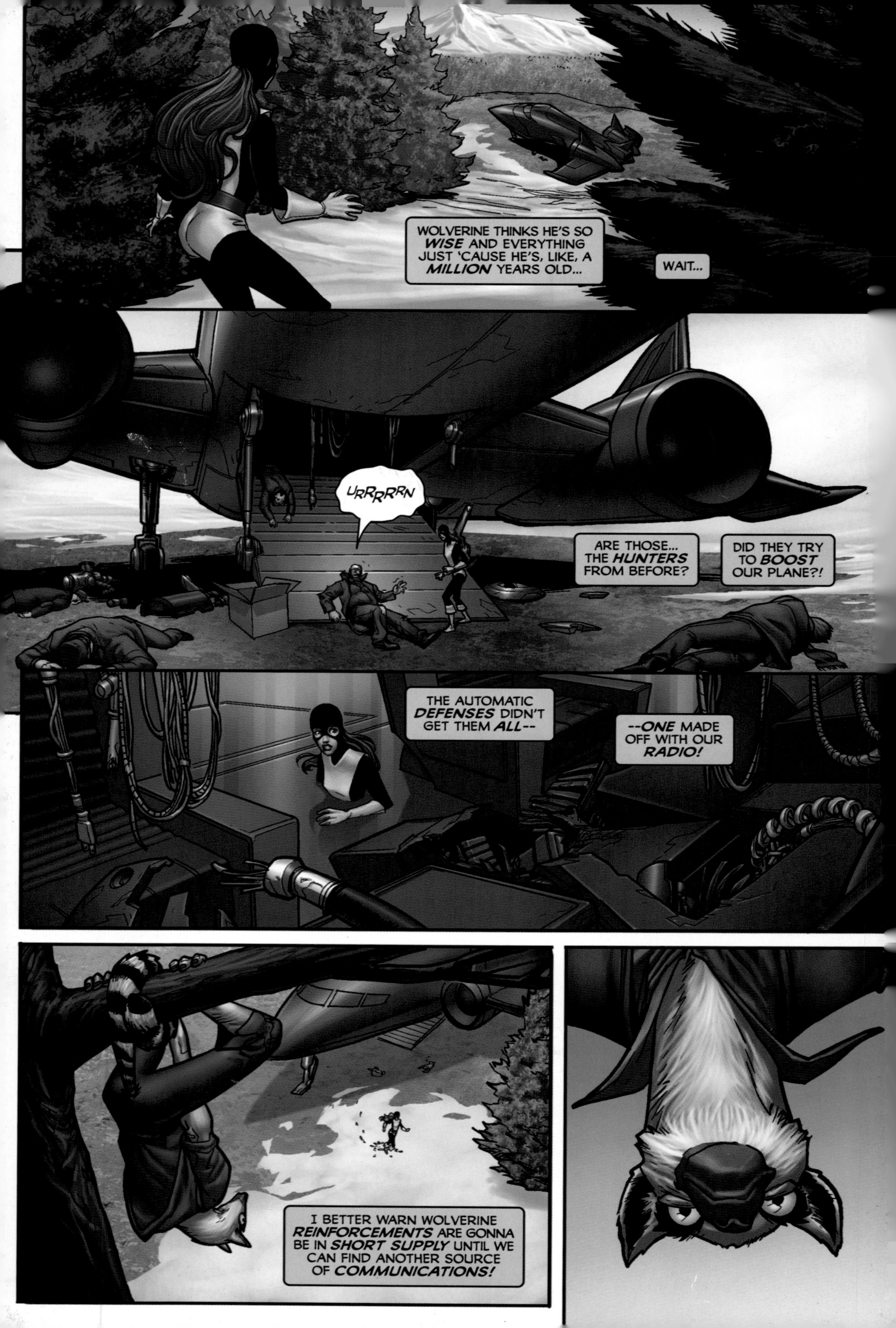
WOLVERINE THINKS HE'S SO WISE AND EVERYTHING JUST 'CAUSE HE'S, LIKE, A MILLION YEARS OLD...
WAIT...
URRRRRN
ARE THOSE... THE HUNTERS FROM BEFORE?
DID THEY TRY TO BOOST OUR PLANE?!
THE AUTOMATIC DEFENSES DIDN'T GET THEM ALL--
--ONE MADE OFF WITH OUR RADIO!
I BETTER WARN WOLVERINE REINFORCEMENTS ARE GONNA BE IN SHORT SUPPLY UNTIL WE CAN FIND ANOTHER SOURCE OF COMMUNICATIONS!

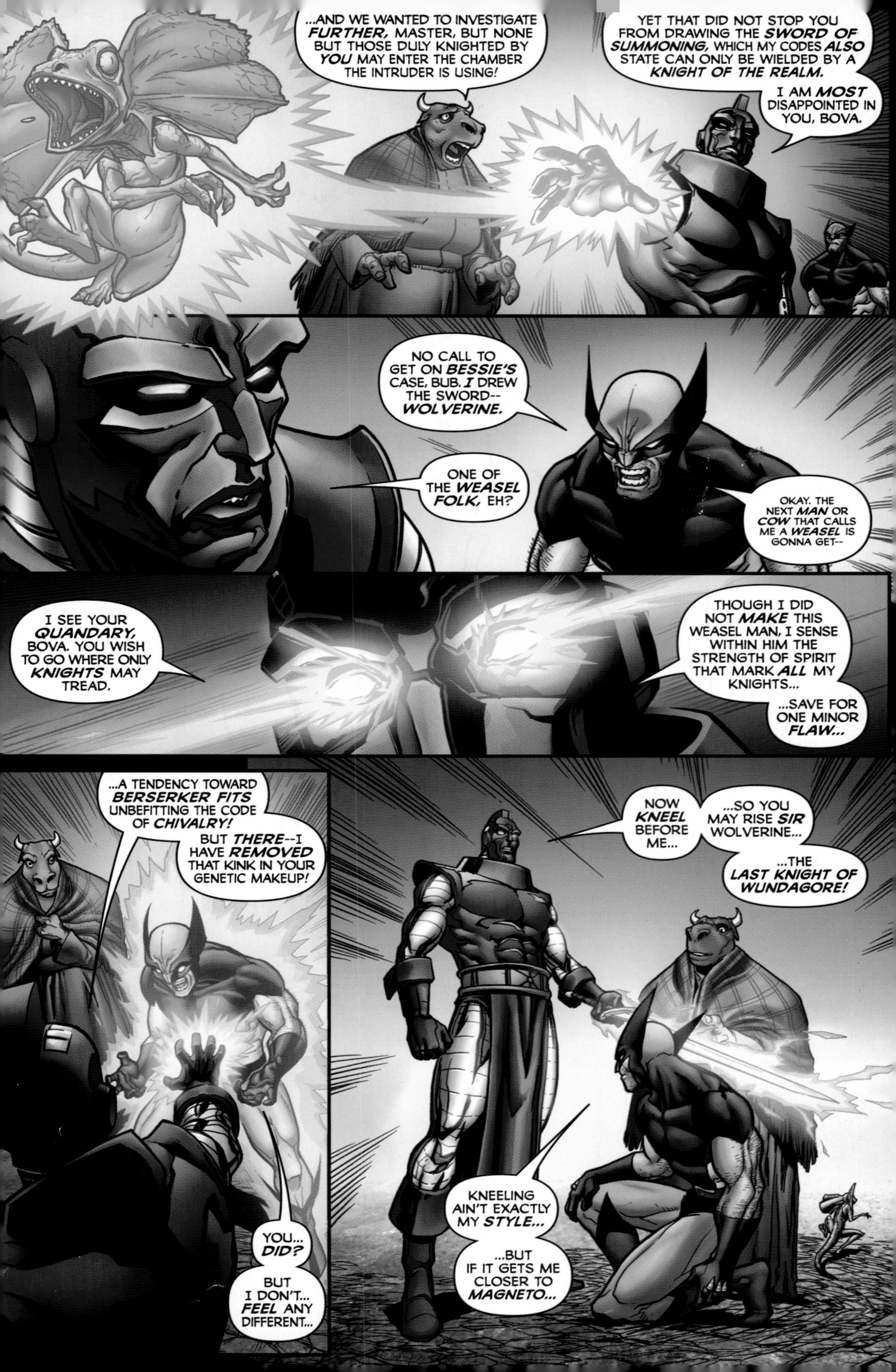

...AND WE WANTED TO INVESTIGATE FURTHER, MASTER, BUT NONE BUT THOSE DULY KNIGHTED BY YOU MAY ENTER THE CHAMBER THE INTRUDER IS USING!
YET THAT DID NOT STOP YOU FROM DRAWING THE SWORD OF SUMMONING, WHICH MY CODES ALSO STATE CAN ONLY BE WIELDED BY A KNIGHT OF THE REALM.
I AM MOST DISAPPOINTED IN YOU, BOVA.
NO CALL TO GET ON BESSIE'S CASE, BUB. I DREW THE SWORD-- WOLVERINE.
ONE OF THE WEASEL FOLK, EH?
OKAY. THE NEXT MAN OR COW THAT CALLS ME A WEASEL IS GONNA GET--
I SEE YOUR QUANDARY, BOVA. YOU WISH TO GO WHERE ONLY KNIGHTS MAY TREAD.
THOUGH I DID NOT MAKE THIS WEASEL MAN, I SENSE WITHIN HIM THE STRENGTH OF SPIRIT THAT MARK ALL MY KNIGHTS...
...SAVE FOR ONE MINOR FLAW...
...A TENDENCY TOWARD BERSERKER FITS UNBEFITTING THE CODE OF CHIVALRY!
BUT THERE--I HAVE REMOVED THAT KINK IN YOUR GENETIC MAKEUP!
YOU... DID?
BUT I DON'T... FEEL ANY DIFFERENT...
NOW KNEEL BEFORE ME...
...SO YOU MAY RISE SIR WOLVERINE...
...THE LAST KNIGHT OF WUNDAGORE!
KNEELING AIN'T EXACTLY MY STYLE...
...BUT IF IT GETS ME CLOSER TO MAGNETO...

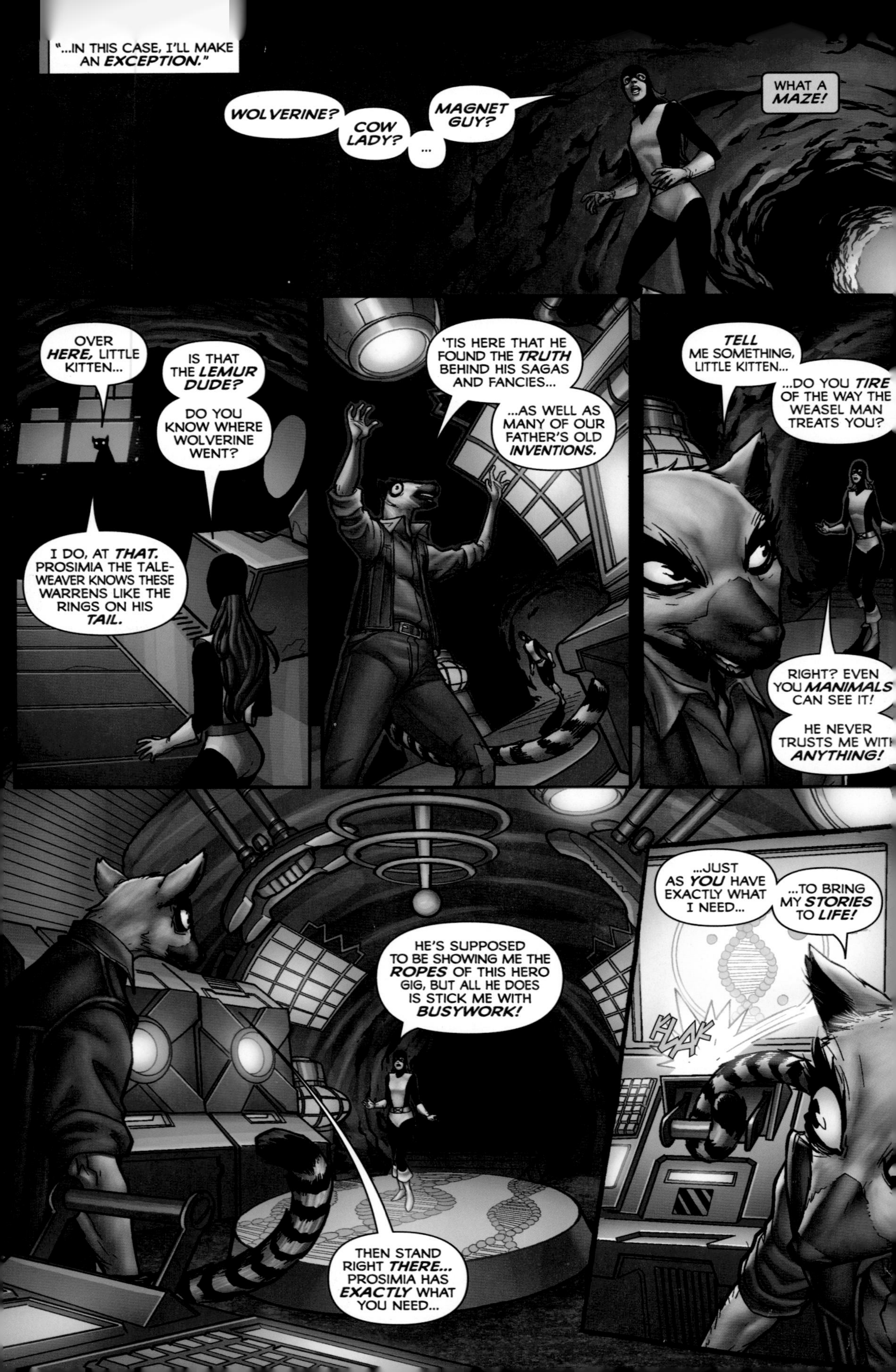
"...IN THIS CASE, I'LL MAKE AN EXCEPTION."
WOLVERINE?
COW LADY?
...
MAGNET GUY?
WHAT A MAZE!
OVER HERE, LITTLE KITTEN...
IS THAT THE LEMUR DUDE?
DO YOU KNOW WHERE WOLVERINE WENT?
I DO, AT THAT. PROSIMIA THE TALE-WEAVER KNOWS THESE WARRENS LIKE THE RINGS ON HIS TAIL.
'TIS HERE THAT HE FOUND THE TRUTH BEHIND HIS SAGAS AND FANCIES...
...AS WELL AS MANY OF OUR FATHER'S OLD INVENTIONS.
TELL ME SOMETHING, LITTLE KITTEN...
...DO YOU TIRE OF THE WAY THE WEASEL MAN TREATS YOU?
RIGHT? EVEN YOU MANIMALS CAN SEE IT!
HE NEVER TRUSTS ME WITH ANYTHING!
HE'S SUPPOSED TO BE SHOWING ME THE ROPES OF THIS HERO GIG, BUT ALL HE DOES IS STICK ME WITH BUSYWORK!
THEN STAND RIGHT THERE... PROSIMIA HAS EXACTLY WHAT YOU NEED...
...JUST AS YOU HAVE EXACTLY WHAT I NEED...
...TO BRING MY STORIES TO LIFE!
KLAK

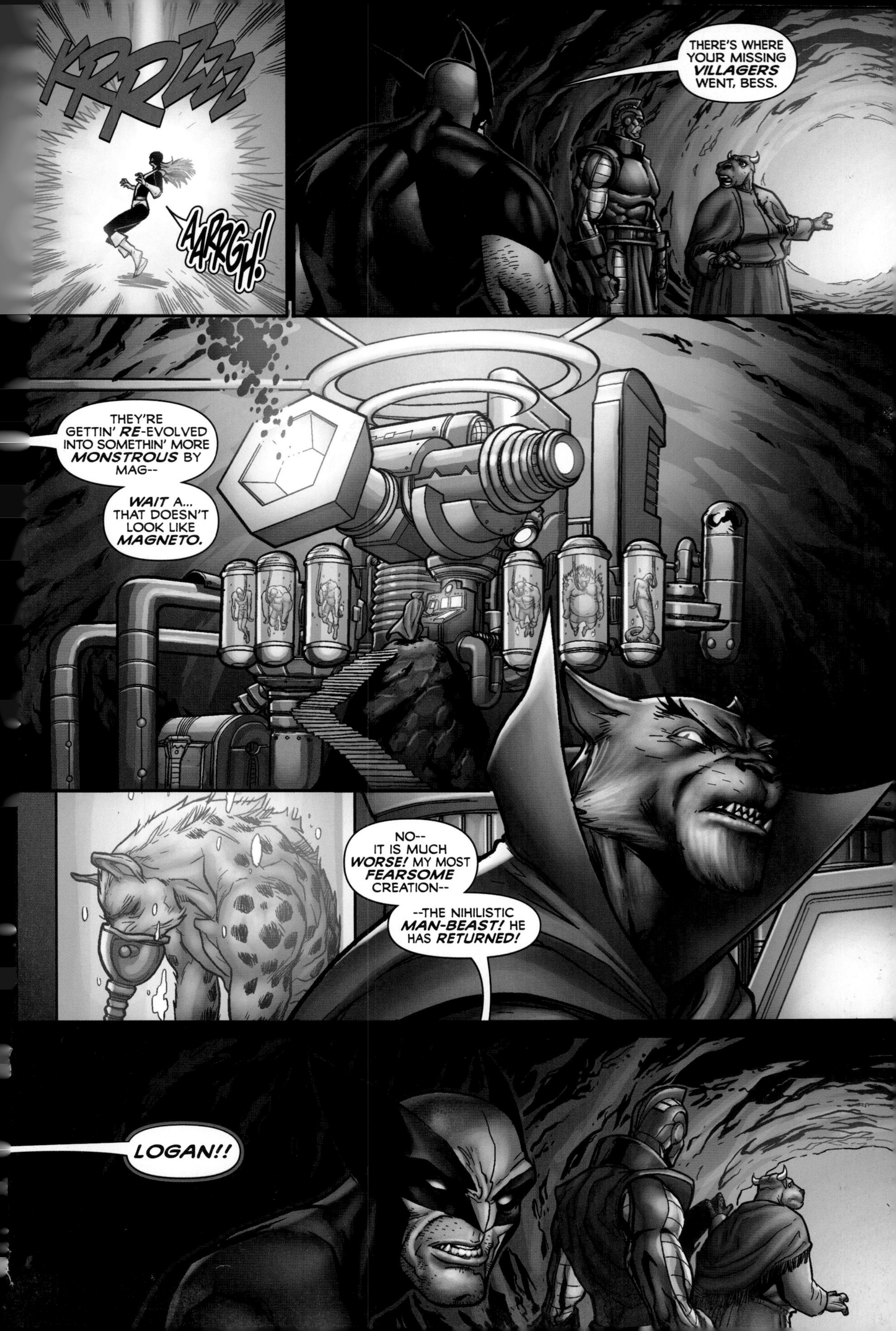
KRRZZZZ
AARRGH!
THERE'S WHERE YOUR MISSING VILLAGERS WENT, BESS.
THEY'RE GETTIN' RE-EVOLVED INTO SOMETHIN' MORE MONSTROUS BY MAG--
WAIT A... THAT DOESN'T LOOK LIKE MAGNETO.
NO-- IT IS MUCH WORSE! MY MOST FEARSOME CREATION--
--THE NIHILISTIC MAN-BEAST! HE HAS RETURNED!
LOGAN!!

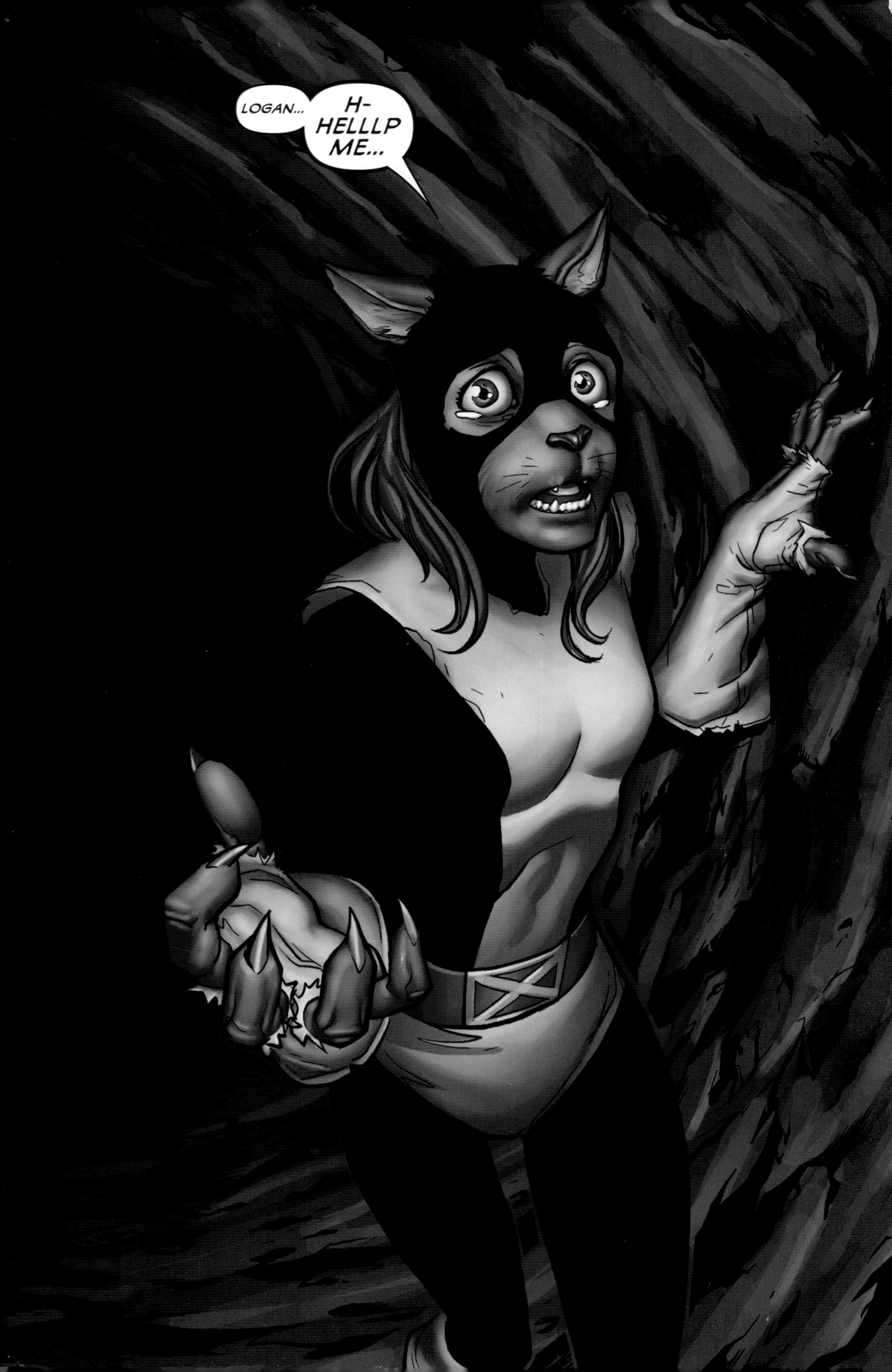

LOGAN...
H-
HELLLP
ME...